Caycie's

Shorts

Tales of Erotic Abandon

Caycie's Shorts

Tales of Erotic Abandon

Caycie Thompson

WBG/WBC Publications
BOWMANVILLE, ON

Published by WBG/WBC Publications
Bowmanville, ON L1C 5C4
www.cayciethompson.com
www.wbgwbc.square.site

Publisher's Note: This is a work of fiction. Names, characters, places, and incidents are a product of the author's imagination. Locales and public names are sometimes used for atmospheric purposes. Any resemblance to actual people, living or dead, or to businesses, companies, events, institutions, or locales is completely coincidental.

Book Layout © 2017 BookDesignTemplates.com
Cover Design: Caycie Thompson

This book is intended for audiences 18+

Caycie's Shorts / Caycie Thompson
ISBN 978-1-7773863-2-0 (paperback)
ISBN 978-1-7773863-3-7 (ebook)

Follow Caycie on her socials
@writtenbycaycie

This collection is dedicated to the Muses.
Without you, there is only the blank page

CONTENTS

Workplace Rendezvous

Behind Closed Doors

I passed by his office and peeked in. I hadn't seen him in a while, and I just wanted to lay eyes on him. If I were being honest, I wanted to lay a lot more than that on him, but I left that to my vivid imaginings.

I saw him, but he didn't see me. He was perched, dressed very professionally, like a schoolboy on the windowsill of his office. It took my breath away. He looked so normal. So approachable. So, human.

I had to pass by quickly, for I didn't want him to see me standing there. But I found myself in need of something at the other end of the hallway. I had to pass by again. My cheeks grew hot as I thought of him sitting there watching the world pass by.

I kept my head down, examining the grain in the carpet as I passed by once more. I fought against my strong desire to look at his door. I did fight. But not all battles can be won. My feet slowed as I approached his door, and I couldn't help but look in.

His voice was quite animated though he sat still on the narrow ledge. The impossibly large window dwarfed him. The largess of his position was comically questioned when framed in this light. And I stood in the hall peering in, adoring him from twenty feet away.

I noticed, a moment too late, that his voice had quieted and when I snapped out of my reverie, I found myself held in the warm embrace of his eyes.

He dipped his chin and looked at me over the rim of his steel frames. His mouth parted slightly, and the pink tip of his tongue wet his lips; and it felt as though all the air was swept out of the room. I was transfixed.

"Come 'ere," he said softly. His lips barely moved as he spoke the words. His lips formed around the words and the sound pulled me into the room, one foot before the other, by the sheer magnetism in his voice. Once I crossed the threshold he smiled. With a controlled twist of his core, he swung his legs off the ledge and stood in front of the window.

"Close the door." His voice was muted but powerful.

It was another command my pounding heart desired to fulfill. He knew what he was doing to me, and he knew I would do anything he desired; he need only ask.

How strange a thing it is to know someone has that kind of power over another.

How intoxicating it must be to wield it.

I stepped into the room and pressed the door closed. The latch engaged with a soft, but final click. We were alone. His position, coupled with a closed door meant that we would not be disturbed, and that knowledge warmed the depths of me.

"I've missed you." His words bathed me in warm honey. They dripped from his sugar sweet lips, and I felt my body begin to hum. I missed him too and there was no denying it.

I stood rooted to the grey berber carpet in the center of the room. He remained at the window, watching me, inquisitive as to what I would do next. But he should know better. I would not take a step further until he reached for me. I couldn't bear the rejection.

He closed the distance between us and I was intoxicated by him. His presence, his cologne, his desire. I watched as he stood before me. The flit of grey in his hazel eyes bespoke of his hunger. His dark lashes accentuated his piercing eyes even further and the steel rim of his glasses framed his face. His jawline was sprinkled with the hint of a five o'clock shadow and his left cheek was pierced with a dimple when he smiled. How I longed to stroke my fingertips along his cheek.

"I've missed you too." I found my voice. It was shy and reserved and it appeared to have an effect on him similar to his on me.

We exhaled; neither of us realizing that we had been holding our breath. Neither of us able to stand the thought of being rejected by the other. The solidarity and security in that knowledge led us closer to one another.

I stepped closer to him, and he met me in the center of the room. I closed my downcast eyes and took in the ethereal shift in the room. He was pure energy. He appeared collected and reserved on the surface, but if I were to only scratch said surface, the entirety of his unbounded sexual appetite. He was in control. It was part of what made him both feared and desired.

I knew it well. Having worked with him professionally off and on for a dozen years I knew that nothing had dulled his rapier wit, his intellect or his cunning, and it was those qualities that I found most desirous.

The electricity between us could not be denied, though we tried. The lingering gazes, the accidental touch of our hands; brushing closely as we passed in the hall – taking in each other's scent - all added heat to a fire that burned slowly and grew in intensity over time. And we find ourselves here, today, before one another, no pretense. With just the fervour of our culminated desire - and a closed door.

⌘⌘⌘⌘⌘

He reached for me. His hand outstretched toward me, and the gold on his finger winked in the mid-afternoon sun that shone through the window. I looked down at it as his long fingers slid gently over my own diamond bands. I blinked; my eyes closed for longer than its usual beat.

"What about-?" I whispered. I could barely hear my own voice and I was desperately hoping he wouldn't answer. It would be my first and only pang of guilt.

In response, he brought my hand to his cheek and closed his eyes tenderly. His proximity overpowered my senses. The silk of his skin in the palm of my hand coursed desire anew through my body as I tenderly stroked his cheek with my thumb.

We stood apart only an arm length, though it felt like a canyon. He took another step forward and turned his lips to the palm of my hand. He reached up and held my hand there. His large hands were strong and assured, and he kept my hand cupped there as he whispered assurances to me. His lips tracing their promises; never once rising to know how they affected the reader or the observer.

In the role of both, I didn't care about the future, I knew one thing. I only needed the here and now with him.

I felt my heartbeat melodically in my chest, and I raised my eyes to meet his. He watched me for a brief moment before he leaned in.

His nose grazed lightly passed mine and he rest his forehead on mine. I felt my heart soar as my hand slipped from his cheek and my fingers delicately traced his ear and slid lightly along his smooth-shaven head.

He looked down at me, his eyes warmed my soul. I felt adored and as I held his gaze, I knew he felt those feelings returned.

He tilted his chin and brought his lips to mine. They were soft and warm. His kiss was yielding and not at all urgent. It was as though we had all the time in the world.

My lips pressed against his as his hands traveled along my arms and pulled me into his strong embrace. His fingers danced lightly on the silk of my blouse and drew lines along my shoulders and across my back, searching for the clasp of my bra.

The tip of my tongue touched his bottom lip, and he pulled me tighter into his embrace. His lips parted, and our tongues met. The fusion of our mounted desire became expressed in a joined sigh and an easing into one another's arms.

Our kiss, once sensuous and slow, had become urgent and heated. And though his mouth was rough on my own pleading lips, his hands were tender as they traced down to my waist and I felt him navigate me through his well-appointed office, narrowly avoiding the chairs his esteemed guest would sit upon as they faced him across the large oak expanse of his desk. He guided me forward toward the window as my mind whirled at the possibilities of our love making.

With each step I felt the gusset of my panties dampen, I had waited so long to feel his body near me. I had imagined what this moment would be like, but I had never expected the depth of my feelings toward him. To feel them returned with each touch of his hand, the pressure of his lips to mine, the depth of his stare, I knew we would savour each moment we had together.

He gripped my hips tight and pulled me against him. The sun's rays penetrated through the window and warmed the room. Our lips were urgent and needful and when his lips left mine for a moment, I felt unmoored.

He looked at me with eyes hooded with desire and leaned his chin in once more. His tongue flicked the tip of my upper lip and sent shivers down my spine. I drew his bottom lip into my mouth and lightly suckled upon it. A faint, delicious moan escaped his lips and when I opened my eyes to look up into his, he was looking at me with wonder.

My hands slipped from his silken shaved head and explored his shoulders. My fingers drew random designs on his back, looping in large circles and ellipses, from his shoulder blades along his well-formed lats, to the small of his back. I brought my dancing fingers along his waist, and I felt his breath draw short as I drew small circles around his belly button, slowly untucking his fine tailored shirt from his impeccably pressed pants.

My thumbs grazed along the front of the flat front of his pants that struggled to contain his growing excitement. My skin tingled with the energy that leapt and sparked between us. There was a subtle shift in the atmosphere, and when I looked into his smoldering eyes, I knew things had changed. It was intoxicating to know that the tables had turned. Now it was I who had the power, and it was he who pined for my touch.

I pressed my lips to his and kissed him hard while my fingers were busy with the nickel rectangular buckle of his belt. The thin black leather strap loosened, and my fingertips brushed along his waist. The tender heat of his flesh fairly sizzled as his abdominal muscles shifted subtly under my fingers. I loved the sound of his quickening breath as his excitement continued to mount.

His hands skated along my arms and tickled my ribs, and I smiled as I felt my heart begin to race. He gently cupped my breasts, and his thumbs mimicked my earlier playful manipulation, as they lightly teased over the sensitive skin of my hardening nipples.

Our tongues dueled, and our hunger was amplified in the closed room. We were enveloped in the moment. His fingers fumbled with the mother of pearl buttons of my slate grey blouse and the sun kissed each inch of my body that was revealed under his touch. My silk blouse drifted to the floor at my feet and his mouth left mine, leaving me breathless.

His eyes, hungry with desire, gazed down at me for a moment, and with his lips he smiled. His eyes were set and cool. It was a look I had seen in his eye before. He was determined, and it was the taking of me that had captured his attention. I would submit to him. I would be his – but on my terms.

His eyes, fixed on their task, blazed a warm trail along my décolletage to the heaving hillocks of my bosom. His hands sculpted my warm breasts and traced along the lace of the black demi-cut material that held the full focus of his attention.

He lowered his lips to my flushed skin. He pressed my mounds together in their lace conveyance and brought his lips to their joined crest and murmured softly. I closed my eyes and savoured the sensation of being worshipped.

The clasp of my bra lay at the base where the lacy material joined under my breasts. With a quick twist of his index and forefinger the clasp came undone and my breasts bounded into his waiting hands. He slid his hands up and along my arms and the black lace joined the crumple of clothing that was quickly growing at our feet.

His lips flowed the path his thumbs had once taken, and he lavished my tender skin with hot kisses. His lips encapsulated each of my nipples in turn and his tongue flicked while his lips suckled, and I felt my clit harden in return.

I stroked the stubble on his cheek and stepped back slightly, my nipple leaving his mouth with an audible pop.

I lifted his head and planted a kiss on his lips. I looked into his eyes and began a trail of kisses that lead from his cheek to his ear. I took in the woodsy scent of his cologne as I kissed his neck and slipped his shirt off his shoulders and planted kisses along his chest, stopping briefly to encircle each of his tan nipples with a flit of my tongue. I lowered to my knees before him and laid a trail of kisses down his stomach to the light happy trail of hair that led passed the open fly of his pants and disappeared underneath the thick white band of his jet-black boxer briefs.

I kissed the tip of his hardened member through the cotton of his briefs and ran my lips over the length of his steel rod. I closed my eyes as I felt his hands brush lightly over my raven hair. I felt his body shift in anticipation as I began to pull on his waistband.

His tumescence sprung free from captivity eager and willing. I licked the tip and slid my tongue along his spongy helmet. Hearing him sigh in delight, I opened my mouth wide to accommodate him and sucked steadily upon his swollen manhood. Alternating between long languid slurping of my mouth to quick directed flicks of the tongue, I had him panting with passion, whispering my name between halted breaths, begging for more. It was intoxicating.

His hips began to thrust slowly, assisting my manual and lingual manipulations to bring him to the brink of ecstasy. His cock, thick and ridged stretched wide my ruby lips and with one final long draw on the straw, I lifted my mouth, leaving him pulsing and quivering before me.

When I stood up before him, my skirt slipped off my shapely hips and joined my blouse at my feet. Clad only in the matching tanga to my black lace bra I beckoned him forward. He kicked off his oxblood loafers and stepped out of his expensive, tailor-made pants and pulled me toward him.

He kissed the lips that had brought him so close and turned me to the window. Pressing my semi-nude bottom to the wide window ledge and he on his knees before me, we traded positions. It was time for him to take the power back and to bring me to heights I had only dreamed.

I looked down at the smooth silk of his hairless head and my fingertips delicately danced along.

His hands smoothed up my legs and grasped the fragile material and pulled them from me. There was no doubt as to my arousal with the gusset soaked through and my lips full and puckered, aching to be claimed by his own.

The first kiss on my soaking quim sent shivers up my spine and a gasp of surprise to escape my lips. His tongue followed suit, seeking out every nook where desire may be unleashed. Within moments and with only the skillful manipulations of his tongue, he had me begging him not to stop. When his lips closed over my swollen bud my eyes grew wide with delight and surprise, but for a moment I was rendered blind. All that existed was the power of the sensations he was creating.

A turbulent sea of ecstasy brewed within me, and I cried out, pulling his face ever tighter against me, his tongue flashing lightning strikes of desire throughout my body.

He rose before me, my eyes unseeing, but all of my senses alert to his every movement and he lifted me at the knees and rested the tops of my quaking thighs on the ledge as he positioned himself to take me fully.

Still in the throes of my orgasm, he pierced his steel rod through my gates. We both cried out. I called to him and scraped my nails down his back as his fingers gripped into my hips harder. He withdrew and crashed through once more. My body stiffened, and my back arched away from the coolness of the glass, and he held me tight as my body succumbed to another intense orgasm, soaking his thrusting member with my juice.

His tool twitched savagely within my depths as he kept his own intense spend at bay. Feeling the vigorous pulse and pull of my quivering pussy subside, he withdrew. Staring down at me for a long moment, he guided his swollen rod to my burgeoning flower and lowered his soft lips to my waiting mouth. He kissed me as he slipped inside. His lips became more insistent as his hips dipped and thrust his tool within my depths.

My cunny sucked and pulsed on his fat prick and my ass raised to meet his heated thrusts. We moved as one, our bodies glistened with sweat and our moans, once muted and our professions of desire and lust, at one time only heard deep within ourselves, now echoed, unbounded, throughout the room.

His pace quickened, and his jizzum-thickened prick deliciously stretched my quim. He reached between us and gathered some of collected moisture and began to draw small tight circles on my sensitive engorged clitty, driving me crazy with desire. I began to babble senselessly, begging him to join me, to explode as I was soon to; to cum deep within me.

He fairly climbed onto the ledge with me, our bodies now turned the length of the window and his right knee resting on the ledge, assisting as a pivot point to drive his spike within me on a delicious angle that sawed across my swollen bud.

Gasping for breath and reaching for one another wildly, we crested the summit. His cock held tight within my pulsing cavern, he moaned deeply, loudly, as his member pulsed jet after jet of his cream into my willing pussy. My honey pot wrung his fat piston, like a hand, greedy to ensure it received every last drop.

We remained poised in the impossible position, half on the ledge, naked and pressed to the glass, and half off, dangling, straining; waiting for the crashes of rapture to ebb and finally dissipate.

He dipped his head and ran his tongue along the hillock of my breast to my lips. His forehead pressed to mine as my nipple began to tighten anew. A pulse crashed through the core of me and gave a loving squeeze to his shrinking manhood. He groaned in response, both lusty and remorseful. I brought my wrist up and glanced at my dainty rose gold watch. It would soon be time to attend to our work.

I gave his cock one last delicate squeeze and placed my lips on his. He kissed me deeply and slowly withdrew. I wrapped him in my arms and hugged him tight.

He pulled me up to sitting and lift me off the ledge. I dressed before him and then watched as he slipped back into his impeccable suit. Looking at him return to the powerful man who commands the respect and admiration of all who knew him made me smile.

As he buttoned up his shirt, I picked up his jacket and removed his pocket square. I pulled down my panties, now soaked with the essence of our joint passion, folded them and placed them in the front pocket of his jacket. He pulled on the jacket and gave me a clit-strumming devilish grin.

He gathered me in his arms and kissed me. His hands ran down my arms and entwined our fingers.

"Tomorrow?" he asked, his voice heavy-laden with longing.

"Tomorrow," I whispered and lay a gentle kiss on his cheek.

I opened the door and walked down the hall to my office. I would see him again before the day was through, but it was to be business as usual.

I watched as he walked past on his way to a meeting, surrounded by admirers and yes-men, and I overheard one comment on his bold choice in pocket square. He smiled and subtly glanced in my direction.

To the unknowing observer, he was carrying a stylish black kerchief, but I knew that every time he turned his head, he would be reminded of our first time, behind closed doors.

Distracted

Originally published in Forbidden: A Temptation Press Anthology

The afternoon sun was lazy in the sky. It hung there beating down its rays on the grey cement below. Unrelenting. Cruel.

I sat, watching the passersby attend to their errands below me. So bored, preoccupied. Lonely. I wonder what they think about as they bustle along. Do they think or is it that they move, almost on autopilot, from chore to chore. Again, boring.

It was hot, too hot for an autumn day, but I guess this is what they are referring to when they talk about global warming. Isn't it? Who are they anyway?

I hear my name and turn my head to the sound. A chill runs up my spine. He's here. The baritone of his voice plays on my skin. I try to play coy, but my body betrays me. I have no choice by to react.

He approaches and I drink him in. His powerfully built frame stands just over 6 feet. His brown hair cut short and playful eyes a blue-green in color. His lopsided smile conveys more than a little mischief.

I turn away from him. I don't want to give away how he affects me. My breath has become shallow, and my pulse quickens with anticipation. Will he touch me? I'm torn. I'm desperate for his touch and though I have never known it, I know that if he doesn't touch me, I will surely die without it.

I don't have to wait long. I sense that he is near me. He closes the distance between us with a few short strides. I feel his breath on the nape of my neck. His scent masculine, patchouli, musk and a touch of sweat. Earthy. Delicious.

His breath is hot on my neck as he steps into me. His hand slides down my arm to my fingers. We entwine our fingers, and he draws our combined hands along my lithe form, my waist to my skirt which rests mid-thigh. Our fingers burning my naked thigh as he delicately traces the hem. His body presses into mine and I feel his yearning.

I turn to face him, my lips parted in anticipation of his mouth. Alas our lips meet. His lips are soft and moist. His breath hot as his claim my lips for his own and I melt into his grasp.

His arms encircle me, and I feel small, vulnerable. Protected. Worshipped.

His hands slide effortlessly across my body as the need rises between us. His lips leave mine and I am breathless.

My fingers fumble with the buttons of his shirt as I try desperately to read the heat of him. I pull off his belt as he helps me out of my shirt. My knees weak as he kisses my neck. His tongue tracing a line to my ear lobe and his kisses his way back down to the exposed flesh of my shoulder, the valley of my neck and I watch in excited frustration as he gently encircles each beast in turn. First the right, then the left and covers them with gentle loving kisses. The tickle of his five o'clock shadow on my tender skin is almost too much to bear. I must have him.

I unzip his jeans and it is clear that he too feels the urgency. Strong hands caress the swell of my buttocks. His thumbs hook under the thin lace of my panties and pulls them down. They lay discarded on the floor, the last barrier to what we need.

His muscular arms raise me up to his waist height. I look down into his eyes. They are no longer playful; they are focused and full of desire. I lean down and capture his lips in a passionate kiss. The top of my tongue touches his and desire, like an electric current, courses through me anew. Held securely in his powerful grasp he braces me against the wall.

Shifting beneath me I feel his rigid manhood against me for only a moment. He presses forward and I gasp. My eyes open in surprised delight. We are one.

I cry out in joy as he takes me. I cling to him as my body sings out praises with every thrust of his hips. I am merely an instrument and he the gifted musician.

As we build to a beautiful crescendo, sweat misting our bodies, marking each other as our own, he whispers my name. His voice thick with desire. It is all I need to send me over the edge, to crest the wall into delirium. I call out to him though so lost in the throes of passion; I am sure he cannot hear me. He feels me though, of this I am certain. He falters once and cries out.

Breathing heavily, sighing, laughing, he sets me down. My long brown hair, usually so neatly tied back is loose and wild, clinging to my face in sexy sweaty pieces. He stands before me, his shirt unbuttoned and damp, his chest muscles glistening. A bead of sweat trails down the hills of his pecs to his navel. I trace the line. Drawing my finger along the river of our combined dampness.

We catch our breath and know that we only have a few moments before our colleagues will enter the conference room. We dress in silence, and he steals away to his post. I am hooked. I knew I would be. The masterful way he held my body. How attentive he was to my needs. I have to have him again. I wondered if he too was thinking of the next time, because there was no doubt, there would be a next time.

I shifted in my seat, the gusset of my panties damp, my nipples strained against my blouse.

"Hey. Are you okay? You look flushed."

Someone is talking to me. I bring my attention back to the room, dragging my eyes from the process servers and workaday shlubs on the grey cement below.

"Hmmm? Yes," I say. "I must have been day dreaming." I look up guiltily. I should at least pretend to be paying attention.

I meet his eye across the conference room table. Does he know? Can he read my mind? Does he have any idea how delicious it would be? Deftly I glide my tongue across my lower lip. A glint of recognition forms in his eye.

I squeeze my thighs together delighting in the dangerous pressure, glance down at my wedding ring and sigh.

Who said business meetings were boring.

I return to my corner office and close the door. Something had to be done about this. He seemed to be everywhere, and it was getting so hard to look at him. So wet to be more specific. He created this fire inside me that was becoming hard to deny and even harder to deny. The way he looked at me during the meeting, it was as though we shared the same fantasy.

I had to stop thinking about him. There was work to do. Burying myself in work was the solution. But then thought of him burying his face between my parted thighs came to mind. My breath hitched in my chest as I imagined him burying his tongue between my folds.

My hand slipped down my body, molding my clothes to my overheated flesh. I reach my treasure trove. My eyes flick toward the door to ensure it is locked. It would not look good if the Chief Information Officer was caught with her hand in the cookie jar. Especially when this cookie jar held delights far more satisfying than an Oreo.

It was far too risky to be doing this in my office, but there was no turning back now. I just had to make sure that when the moment hit, I could stifle my cry. Sensation after sensation crashed through my mind as I pictured his young, luscious body positioned below mine, his mouth busily bringing me nearer and nearer to climax.

My finger strums firmly across my too sensitive button and I soar. Quickly I bring my hand to my mouth to cut off the sound. The sound of panting abounds in the enclosed office. My orgasm is short lived, but it was powerful. I sit in my high back leather chair and try to catch my breath. I have to stop doing this at work. Someone is bound to walk in one of these days.

It had been too long since I had a man touch me the way I needed to be touched.

There was an otherness to being a widow. People did not seem to know what to say to you. The first year was incredibly difficult. I had become so isolated. With the kids gone off to school and their own lives, I was very much on my own. And for a long time that was all right. I took care of myself, ate right, exercised. All of the things you are supposed to do. I had even tried to get back out there once or twice at the not too subtle urging of girlfriends, but I wasn't ready to give up that place in my heart that was strictly reserved for my husband.

It wasn't until Charlie started with my firm that I had even felt remotely interested in a man. And what I felt for him was far more than interest. He lit a fire in me that kept me awake at night. I thought that those days were long behind me, though only being 51 I don't know why I had rationalized it quite that way.

He was a magnificent specimen. He was tall and finely built. He was an exceptional IT professional who specialized in security and I admired his intellect, but it was his strong hands, his carefully groomed five o'clock shadow, his sculptured shoulders that held my attention when he came into the room. I watched him while he spoke, embarrassed to admit that I rarely heard what he said as I was captivated with the curve of his sensuous lips. I often thought of those lips on my body. My lips on his body. He made me wet.

There was only one problem; he was just a couple of years older than my son.

I fix my skirt and give myself a once over before I open my office door. I walk to the washroom and stare into the mirror at my reflection. My hair hangs in tight curls and frames my still somewhat flushed face. I wash my hands and pat my face with a cool damp paper towel. Only a couple of hours left until the end of the day. I can make it.

Once I return to my office I pour myself a glass of water and turn my attention back to my monitor.

A sharp rap at the door pulls my eyes from the email I had been reading.

"Come in," I called. Charlie's supervisor, Loretta, stands in the doorway. "Hey, Loretta. What's up?"

"I was just wondering when you needed the reports pulled for the incidents we attended to over the month."

Loretta pauses for a moment and then continues. I suppose the look on my face was enough to convey to her that I had no idea to what she referred.

"In the meeting," she began. "The director wanted reports from each sector to send up to headquarters."

Loretta twisted her mouth impatiently. I hate when she does that.

"Right," I respond. "Um, if I could get them first thing tomorrow that would be great. I have a one-on-one meeting with her tomorrow at 10 o'clock."

"That would mean that someone would have to stay tonight to get it done."

"Yes, Loretta, I suppose it would."

"Okay, well, I am not able to stay tonight to assist with this project. I guess will canvas my team to see who is available to work this evening."

"Yes, that would be good. If you could find one or two people to work tonight, it would be greatly appreciated."

"Sure, I will ask. But I would be surprised if I could find two." Loretta said dismissively and walks out of the room.

"Thank you, Loretta," I said to her receding form and turn back to my monitor. I shake my head at the interaction. She could be a lot to handle, but she was a good tech.

The remainder of the day had passed by quickly and without incident.

A knock on my door brings my attention to my doorway. This time it was not Loretta's perpetually disappointed face looking back at me. A warm smile spread across my lips.

"Hi guys!" I said, with probably a little too much excitement in my voice. In my door stood Pamela and Charlie.

"Hey Boss," Pamela said. "We heard you were looking for volunteers to stay to help get those reports out?"

"Yeah. You are both available?" I asked, fixing my eyes on Pamela as I was afraid my eagerness would betray me if I caught Charlie's eye.

"Well, I am free for an hour or so, but I have to take off after that. But Charles, here, is at your disposal. All night, if need be," Pamela responded and shot Charlie a quick look and then rested her gaze on me.

Was I mistaken? Did she just make a comment laced with innuendo? I can't be that out of touch to have missed it. And I thought I saw Charlie's cheeks flush a bit. I would not dare acknowledge it.

"Okay! That's great," I said. "Well, there is no shortage of data to pull and organize, so let's get started, shall we?"

Pamela came into my office a short time later to advise that she was leaving but that her analytics were complete. She placed her report on my desk and walked out of my office. She turned back and said, "I'll send Charlie in, so you two can make sure you are on the same page."

Okay, what was that about I asked myself. Had she seen the way I was looking at him in the meeting earlier? I had always been so careful around him. I didn't want to look like a cougar ready to pounce on a younger man. I hoped Charlie didn't see it that way.

Charlie came into my office about 15 minutes later. He had a report in his hand as well.

"Done for the night?" I asked. I hoped that he wasn't, but I wouldn't make him stay if he wanted to leave.

"No, I just wanted to give you this before I started to work on the last one."

"Oh. Okay. No problem." There was a strange energy in the room.

Charlie placed the report on my desk and lingered there for a moment. I looked at the folder and his hand. The thickness of his fingers and how they so innocently perched on the folder. I was entranced by them.

I looked up to see he was watching me. Curious. He had the same look that graced his face at the meeting.

"Uh, how about we order some dinner in? We might be here a while yet." My offer was selfish, but it might entice him to stay a bit longer.

"Dinner sounds great."

Charlie sat down in the chair opposite my desk. His brown eyes fixed on mine. I felt a familiar heat rising within me. If he only knew what he did to me.

"I want to apologize for Pam's comments earlier. I could see that it made you a little bit uncomfortable. And who knows what she said when she was in here earlier." Charlie laughed.

Was he nervous? Around me? He had never acted that way before.

"I wasn't uncomfortable. A little innuendo never hurt anybody. Pamela's just like that I guess," I chuckled in response. "Okay, so, what shall we have for dinner?"

I stand up and walk around my desk. Charlie is watching my every move. He is the one prowling. I can hardly believe it.

As I walk past him, he shifts subtly in his chair. The back of his hand grazes my leg as I pass. I slow for a moment, then continue to the cabinet where I keep the menus.

He stands and joins me at the cabinet and takes the stack from my hand, places it on the round table where, in the morning, I would have the meeting with my boss. He was so close to me. The smell of his cologne overpowering rational thought. I turn to face him, my body teeming with desire.

"I hope I am not out of line when I say I saw that look you gave me in the conference room today. I liked it."

"Oh?"

"Yeah."

I shudder as Charlie slides his hand up my arm and pulls me closer to him. My chest is pressed to his. His hand turns my face to his and his lips graze mine.

"I have wanted to do this for a long time. It wasn't until today that I knew you felt the same way."

I feel his lips slide sensuously over mine as he speaks. My knees are weak as he continues.

"I have been craving an opportunity like this for a long time. To be alone with you. Pamela knows that. Hence the comments earlier. I hope this is not too forward, but I haven't been able to think of anything else since the meeting today."

Before I can respond Charlie slides his tongue along my bottom lip. I melt into his embrace and part my lips to allow him access. He draws me closer in his arms and backs me up to the cabinet. My mind is rushing. I can feel the heat from his body radiating from him like a furnace. I kiss him back. I stroke my tongue along the bottom of his. The tips of our tongues clash together. The sound of my soft whimpers fills my office. My hands slide down his body. They are urgent and seeking. I am too hot to consider romance. I need him inside me. I need him to pleasure me.

Without speaking he recognizes my craving. His hands reach under my skirt and he slips his finger along the lacey material of my panties to the soaked cotton. A groan of approval echoes in his throat. I sigh and lean my head back as he tastes the delicate skin of my neck. His finger slips past the cotton and gently sweeps along my sensitive swollen lips. He turns me toward the couch and gently guides me onto my back. I watch, entranced, as he pushes my skirt up, the material gathered at my waist, and he lays heated kiss upon kiss up the suppleness of my thighs.

He draws my panties down. My neatly trimmed mound exposed to his gaze, his touch. With deft fingers, he explores. His fingers becoming slippery as they slide through my wetness.

He leans forward, and I hold my breath. When his lips finally touch me, I am in heaven. He draws one lip in at a time, sucking for a moment and then onto the next. His tongue tapping the root of my heat. He pushed my thighs apart and held them firmly. He attached his suckling lips to my clit and held on. Pleasure burst through me. I felt my orgasm rushing forward. I could not hold back. My fingers comb through his hair.

"Charlie," I whimpered. Calling his name seemed to make him hotter, seemed to make me hotter. I tried to close my thighs around his head, but his arms held me open to his delicious assault. He began to flick my clit with his tongue and stars danced before my eyes.

"I'm cumming," I cried. My fingers, entwined in his hair, I held him to my orgasming cunny. My breath came in short intense gasps as his tongue ravished my delicate button. His face drenched from the amount of juice my pussy squirted in response to his masterful touch. I could barely catch my breath.

My eyes blinked open. Charlie was standing naked before me, his tumescent member proudly before him. I could not have imagined a more perfect sight. I lick my lips and raise up on my elbows. He is beautiful. My imagination did not do justice to his physique. The peaks and valleys of his muscular arms, the breadth of his shoulders, the happy trail that led from his belly button to his fabulously thick manhood.

I stand and wrap my hand around his thickness. I can feel his heartbeat in the meaty tool, and I can no longer wait to feel it crash through my gates and bring me to the peaks of pleasure. Luckily for me, Charlie seems to be one step ahead.

Kissing me passionately, I taste myself on his lips. Spicy and tart. I push my skirt down over my hips and fight with the buttons on my shirt to remove it. Charlie expertly unhooks my bra, and my pillowy breasts spill forth.

Leaning me against the table, he brings his mouth down to my nipples in turn, sucking them and playfully biting them to long, hard peaks.

Without warning, Charlie turns me around. His face buried in my tight curls I feel his hardness across my buttocks. A trail of pre-cum marks his sensuous path. I lean forward on the table and part my thighs. Murmuring to him, he positions himself between my quaking thighs.

"Take me," I utter. I feel him slide the bloated head along my pouting lips and slowly enter me. I gasp as I feel him slip inside. He moves slowly as he sinks inch after inch into my burning honeypot. My pussy ripples around his hard cock as each inch of him causes mini orgasms to shoot through me.

He pulls back just as slowly; I don't know how much of this delicious torture I can take. His strokes are so deliberate. I can only mewl my approval, I have lost the ability to speak.

His left hand strokes my hip and grabs my leg. He raises my ankle to his hip and holds it there. I sucked in a deep breath as he bottomed out inside me, his balls resting on my engorged clit. His right hand holds my right hip and I feel him draw back. I cry out as he slams into me. His hand on my hip holds me in place, while his other hand holds me open. I feel his balls tickle my clit on every stroke. His cock brushing against my g-spot causes my knee to buckle, but he holds me tighter bringing me quickly to earth shattering release. My cunny squeezes him, and I hear his breath quickening. His pace is unrelenting as he comes closer. The sound of our bodies slapping together is music. My soaking cunt sucking on his dick urges him to release and he cries out. The warm splashes deep inside me, the feeling of his strong hands holding me, of the intense sensation my clit was experiencing thrust me into another mind blanking orgasm.

My body shuddered beneath him as he lay on top of me, our orgasms subsiding. As Charlie pulls out, my nerve endings light up anew and I smile.

Turning around, I kiss him. I draw a finger along his wet and sticky cock and bring it to my lips.

"We had better order some food. It's gonna be a long night."

I was right about one thing in my daydream. Without a doubt there would be a next time.

The Lift

The elevator in my office building is one of the least reliable contraptions ever designed. It is never a good idea to get inside without your cellphone – though reception in there is spotty at best, so calling for help is useless. It merely serves as a form of entertainment while you wait to be rescued.

I climbed inside, not thinking much of my usual ride from the 15th floor to the lobby. It was the end of the day, and I wanted nothing more than to go home.

The elevator stopped on the ninth floor and in stepped on of the most beautiful men I had ever seen. I had noticed him in the building before. He was relatively new. Always impeccably dressed. Always in a suit, but never a tie. His piercing blue eyes were a stark contrast to his jet-black hair. Those eyes were framed by thick, dark eyelashes that you could not help but notice.

For whatever reason, he seemed terribly shy. He couldn't hold eye contact for any length of time. We had exchanged casual smiles on occasion and brief hellos, but that was the extent of our interaction. I had often wondered if it was me who made him feel that way, but I would quickly put that idea out of my mind. He was probably like that with everyone.

He rarely spoke, outside of those brief exchanges we would have in the elevator, but every time he did, the tenor of his voice strummed directly on my clit.

Just being around him made my mind go to places that brought heart to my cheeks. I wanted him. I wanted to teach him things. Ways to make my body soar with pleasure. But I also did not want him to see that in my eyes, here in this enclosed space. So, I pulled out my phone and creased my forehead in concentration over a fictional engaging text conversation.

The elevator doors closed, and we were alone. It was all I could do to keep my eyes on my phone as the wood panel box descended.

I kept looking in his direction and on one of those occasions met his eyes.

In that moment we smiled at each other, both caught in the glances we had snuck towards one another, we felt as though the earth rattled.

I hopped into his arms in fear. The damned elevator had come to an abrupt halt in its descent. And while we were all most certainly aware that it had the tendency to do this, I had yet to find myself caught inside when it did.

"I'm sorry," I breathe and put my hand flat on his chest.

"No need to apologize," he said and held me tight against his body.

He was warm. Heat radiated off his chest and, like a lit candle, the scent of him wafted through the enclosed space.

He smelled clean and masculine. I must admit, I swooned for a moment.

My eyes found his again and the corner of his eyes crinkled with a smile and his hands tightened on my hips, drawing me closer to him.

I could feel the heat of his body radiate through mine and what's more, I could feel the stiffness forming in his pants.

I sighed contentedly and melted into his embrace.

"I've never been stuck before,' I confessed. "Have you?"

"No," he admitted. "But from what I have heard, we might be in here for a while."

He peered down at me with a familiar look. It, undoubtedly, was a look of hunger, but somehow, it was not presumptuous. It was very alluring. Both vulnerable and wanton. His blue eyes examined mine for the slightest hint of hesitation as I returned his hungry gaze.

I gave him no reason to hesitate, but to ensure he knew I was very interested, my hand slipped down his chest and settled on the buckle of his belt.

He drew a deep breath and held it for a moment. His excitement was clear, and I felt his heat pulse rising from him in waves.

His hands smooth along the sides of my skirt and floated over the roundness of my ass. I felt my panties dampen as he massaged my globes and held my lustful stare.

Turning my face upwards to face him, he tilted his downwards to meet my lips in a fiery kiss. His tongue, thick and electric, slid along my lips. A silent request. My lips parted and my tongue lightly met his. An invitation to continue.

I was overwhelmed by him. His tongue lashed along my own, along the roof of my mouth, sparking electricity to flood through my body and concentrate its effects along the pouting lips of my cunny which, by now, had completely saturated the gusset of my panties.

He gathered the material of my skirt into his hands as he drew it higher up my thighs.

My heart raced against my chest as cool air graced my upper thighs. My thigh high stockings remained in place. His fingers slid along the lacy material and grazed along my tender skin.

While engaged in our delicious kiss, I drew my fingers along his waist. Pressed against him, there was no doubt about his excitement.

My fingers set to work on his belt and in a trace his pants were open, and his turgid member peeked out the top of his designer briefs.

I loved to hear his sharp intake of breath as the cool air of the elevator touched the tip of his cock, wet with pre-cum.

My thumb swiped along the tip to gather his offering and in response, his tongue plunged deeper into my willing mouth. Our tongues sparked and fluttered against one another, sending jolts of excited energy through my body, making me crave more.

He drew his index finger along my thigh, tracing it to my sopping treasure.

I withdrew from the kiss, breathless, tingling, and looked into his eyes. He gazed back with wanton desire and hooked his thumbs on the delicate waistband of my panties and dragged them downward.

I stepped out of them and sighed as his hands drew up the inside of my thighs to my naked quim.

My own hands worked quickly to free him completely. I stroked him slowly, deliberately as his hands hungrily investigated my nakedness. His hands were deliciously rough against the softness of my buttocks. He kneaded them with increasing urgency while his lips feasted hungrily upon my own.

Our breathing was laboured as our excitement mounted. A delighted gasp escaped my lips as his fingers travelled along the honeyed petals of my yearning flower, tickled my surging bud and slipped through to my inner heat.

My hips began to surge and flow with his manual manipulations. I was enjoying the teasing sensation of my slow building orgasm.

My own manual manipulations of his turgid member became more insistent. I needed to feel his powerful tool in my heated depths.

He was in tune with my animal passions, and both aware we didn't know when *help* would appear, we wanted to make the best use of our time together.

I dragged my teeth along his plump lower lip and drew my hips backward. I loved the sensation of his thick fingers being pulled from my tight quim.

I pulled his hot tool toward me and his hands, sticky with my juice, planted my hips to the back wall of the elevator.

He lifted my skirt and looked down at my dampened pussy and smiled appreciatively. He stepped forward and closed the space between us.

His throbbing manhood, having a mind of its own, tapped, unassisted, against my pouting lips.

He lowered himself slightly and properly lined up our steaming sex. He angled his hips beneath mine and slowly, deliciously, raised them to meet mine.

His cock crested my slick lips and he held himself there, just inside the gates of my treasure trove, for one long, incredible moment. We signed in unison as he lowered his hips and slipped out of my pouting, sucking lips and lifted them to enter me again. He made me craven with desire as his fat helmet just pushed beyond my gates and popped out again. My thirsty lips grabbed his juicy helmet and sucked on him. The sensation was dizzying.

It was too delicious an appetizer to last for long. On his next languid thrust, my hips lowered to meet his. His prick pierced through and plunged into my depths.

His eyes locked with mine and with a firm grasp on my hips, he pulled back and thrust deeper.

My eyes widened with surprise as he angled his steel cock to slide deliciously against my sweet spot. I whimpered with desire and our pace quickened.

His hips moved as a piston. A derrick with a single purpose, to reach the crest and loosen the explosion of liquid fire within.

I threw my arms around his neck, and he lifted me into his strong arms. I raised my legs and wrapped my ankles around his busily moving, muscular hips.

Our heated cries chorused together; crashed and bounded from wall to wall in the small conveyance.

He was getting close. I could feel his thick prick becoming fuller, fatter, as it wedged between my slackened, dripping lips and sawing along my swollen button. He brought me along with him as he rapidly hammered his jizzum-ridged prick, mere moments from achieving our sole mutual purpose.

Engaged as we were, the faint static crackle in the background did not alert us to the interruption.

Exclamations of "Yesses", as his derrick found liquid gold answered the question security had posed.

Were we all right? Yes, I'd say we were!

Gasping for breath between lusty sighs and chuckles, we slipped down to the floor and lay, cuddled close, awaiting our rescuers.

Close together, we teased each other. My hand formed into a light fist and pulled tenderly on his semi-hard prick, while his digits slid playfully along my oversexed and pouting lips.

When the doors finally opened, we thanked the firefighters and, blushing passed security, we took our leave. We needed to find a place to put out the flame we had reignited.

Now, whenever he and I happen to be in the elevator together, the weight of our exchanged glances is enough to set the lift and everyone aboard alight.

I, for one, can't wait to get stuck again.

Short & Sizzlin'

On Principal

"The Principal will see you now."

I nodded to the secretary and smoothed my hands down my skirt.

Getting called to the office was exciting.

He stood; his turgid spear still smeared with lipstick from another.

My clit pulsed.

"One week's detention." His opening bid.

I splayed my hands upon the desk and glanced at him over my shoulder.

He pushed the flowing fabric aside, exposing my pouting, needful sex; and in one motion, he took me fully.

My back arched as we crashed toward ecstasy.

"No detention," I panted.

Spent, he agreed.

The things parents do for their kids.

Seize the Day

The salt of your skin is bright on my tongue
Your excited body hums in return
I drink you in and am rewarded by delicious pearls
Whetting my furtive imagination

Arched and ready, explosion imminent
I entwine myself with you
Feeling the very Earth quake beneath my yielding form

Eyes locked, my name caught mid-call on your tongue
Your lips formed, tantalizing
Your hands firm upon my sides

Nary room between us for air
For sweat
For the drippings of pleasure

You rise from beneath
Primal and Hungry
Desperate and Howling
Releasing pure ecstasy

Your body calls to me
And I respond
A language spoken only between us
Understood only by us

I answer, singing your name to the Heavens
For only they know true bliss
Quivering and Gasping
Satiated and Gleeful

Wrapped in one another, we rest
For as dawn breaks, so too, do you rise
Inspired to seize the day
And love every hot, aching moment

The Fair's In Town

When I moved back to the small town where I grew up, years after my folks had moved away, it was for many reasons. One of those reasons being, there was no event quite like the County Fair.

Living in the city for as long as I had, I really missed the sights, sounds, and smells of a true county fair. Corn roasting, kids screaming on the Tilt-A-Whirl and the amusing distorted images of the House of Mirrors.

I loved the House of Mirrors. It showed you for who you really were. Beautiful, Ugly. Depraved.

I often recall my experiences in the House of Mirrors as ones of great pleasure. One after hours dalliance taught me the true, raw nature of the carnival. That delicious summer night in my youth opened my eyes, and I learned the real fun on the midway happens after dark.

One such memory quickens my pulse and dampens my panties every time.

There was no greater thrill than to be inside, after hours, stripped down to nothing but ankle socks and runners, and watch my lover, whomever he happened to be that night, advance from a direction I could not readily discern.

His long, thick cock preceding him as seven of him became five, then three, and then finally one. The many versions of him converging into one and then he was there before me. His member pointed at me, like an angry teacher.

It was both a searing accusation and a delicious promise.

I knew I was responsible. My pert breasts tingled, and my eyes were wide with anticipation.

We were gonna fuck.

It was both penance and salvation for the generic sins of youth.

He turned me around and pressed me to the mirror. His hot flesh against mine and I could feel the size of his prick against the plumpness of my ass. He moved his hips and slid his cock along the cleft of my round globes. He held himself there for a long, delirious moment while the heat of our breath fogged the cool reflective surface and obscured our view.

I no longer needed to see. My other senses had awakened and became as one. I gasped as I felt the crest of his turgid shaft part my dewy lips and crash into me.

He raised my ankle to his hip and rocked his hips forward to enter me deeper. With a slow twist of his hip, he screwed his fat rod into my tight canal. He rested his forehead on the nape of my neck and commented on how cute my little socks were. Tilting his hips directly below mine, he pistoned upwards. Pressing deeply, he filled me. I arched back, and he captured my earlobe between his teeth, then licked the sensitive inner ridge sending chills along my spine.

His breath was hot on my neck, and my slavering pussy clenched his fat prick in response, holding it in my silken glove, wringing it and sucking on it with my pouting sopping lips.

Sweat slicked surfaces and fingerprints told the tale of our movements through the mirrored halls. Lipstick here and droplets of overflowing juice there, the House of Mirrors was where, with tits pressed to the glass and his cock ramming me hard, I shook the walls with a thunderous climax.

The intoxicating sound of his cum-soaked flesh slapped against mine, the delicious wet of our shared juices sullied my flushed skin.

We were sweaty and sated, and I loved every second of it.

The fair brings with it the promise of seven days full of candy floss and amusement and seven nights of sweet, sticky debauchery.

Next week, the fair is coming back to town, and my depraved pussy will be the first in line for a ticket.

A Blissful Reunion

Absence may make a heart fond
But in this moment,
It is surely not my heart that aches

His strong arms, broad chest
Shoulders meant to anchor –
Fingernails [a sigh], Ankles [a gasp], Knees [so deep]

Lips, plump, heated. Incredible.
His tongue – electric and sweet
Mind-blowingly talented

A mere kiss hello
My body rises to meet him
Hips and breasts leading the way

With one look
Reduces me
To but a quivering mass of wanton desire

His powerful hands embrace me
Suddenly I am small, feminine
My heart quickens

I feel his excitement
Hot and turgid
Wresting against cloth to be freed

Tumbling into my hands
I smooth his steel
Eyes wide with anticipation

My mouth hungry
Lips wrapped, tongue coiled
Wet, constant, thrilling

Clothes stripped away
In his rugged and careful hands
I am Worshipped

His tongue – in a word, Gifted
Stirring, satisfying
Sets me ablaze

Posed beneath his untamed instrument
My glistening lips pout
Ready to receive him

Exposed and trusting, we move as one
Surrendering to the thrust and piston
To the arc and sway

Rewarded by whimpers and growls
Breath from blistering to deliberate
A chorus rises between us

Teeth nip at necks
Fingers twist in satin
We are sweat-drowned – Sated

Together, we are passion
All consuming and trembling
Delirious

When he goes, I will miss him
When he calls, I will come [again and again]
Until our next blissful reunion

Taut Strings

I feel like the strings of his guitar. Taut and yet, yielding. Music locked away deep inside, yearning to be set free by the hands of a man skilled in the art of desire.

The song begins, and from the first bars, I am transported. I look up to the ceiling. It feels as though he is playing just for me. I can feel his passion in every strum of the strings. When he begins to sing, I am already gone. Lost in my sweet imaginings.

I have no choice, I am drawn in. I allow myself to surrender.

I can feel his heat, his presence, beside me. The brush of his lips on my neck. The skill of his fingers directly on my moist and sensitive flesh.

He hasn't touched me, yet I give myself to him freely. My hands are his. They slide over my tender skin, covering it in playful pinches and pulls, sparking my desire, bringing me closer to him. Closer to paradise.

My hips lift and twist to his rhythm. My chest rises and falls in sync with his skillful manipulations on the tense metal strings. Finally, my breath catches, and I erupt. Exaltations in tune with the triumphant crescendo.

Cries of ecstasy quiet to soft whimperings. I am spent. But not yet satisfied.

The album is on repeat, and I will surrender to him again and again before sleep takes me and I dream of delightful ravagings.

Sounds of the Season

It's the most wonderful time of the year. The song is right, but the reason I feel that way has nothing to do with jingle bells and certainly nothing to do with silent nights.

My nights have been anything but silent, filled with laughter and conversation, and most wonderful of all, the delectable sounds of pleasure. My days and nights have been filled with the sound bodies make when they slap together, covered in sweat and mutual juices.

The prelude to the upcoming symphony is delightful. The pop of a button and the grate of the zipper; the tinkle of his metal buckle and the whoosh of leather as I pull the belt from his waist builds the anticipation to hear the clatter of the belt and the rustle of denim hit the bedroom floor.

Hard and gleaming, peeking over the waistband of his cobalt-coloured boxer briefs, the instrument is ready to be played and I, its artist, am eager for the performance to continue so I can display my skills.

He calls me "Angel" as I pull down the fine textured garment and he is naked.

Glorious.

I, on my knees before him, stare up at his mighty instrument. I hear the familiar refrain swell within me. One of pained pleasure. Aching anticipation. It is joyous.

I look beyond the ridged bow and gaze into his eyes as I plant a kiss on the tip.

We will make sweet music.

The bed creaks as I lay him down. The overture.

The sound of excited sighs as I lick the tip of his hard cock and playfully drag my teeth along his shaft; the satisfying sound of his intake of breath as I take the heft of his sac in my hand, tickle my fingernails along his sensitive skin and feel his balls shift and roll in their tight pouch.

There is the faint jingle of my dangling earrings as my mouth encircles him and, along with my hands, my lips slide down his tumescence and back up again to swirl my tongue around his bloated helmet and back down again.

The delightful sound he makes when I take his thick shaft deep, and the tip of his pulsing knob touches the back of my tongue, just before I take him down my tight throat.

The harmonious sound of two lovers as we play through the first movement; the slow suck and slurp along his rigid tool and his guttural moans chorus throughout the room.

All these sounds culminate with the sound of his halted voice as he, at first breathless, whispers my name. Those whispers become urgent, louder, breathier, and desperate until he can no longer hold back.

The crescendo, the apex of the performance, is celebrated with great arcs of jizzum that race passed my pink tongue and ruby lips and splash on the aubergine sheets below.

From the crashing growl deep in his chest to the mewling diminuendo that reverberates, he regains his breath for he knows that this symphony has four parts, and this is only the first movement.

Lust At First Sight

Peace Be With You

The bells chime and a voice echoes through the chamber, signalling when to move from posture to posture. Mass was an important part of Felicity's weekly spiritual re-set. After the week she had, she needed a cleanse. Still, she sat at the end of the pew in the third row from the back, just in case she got her fill and needed to slip out unnoticed.

Felicity was joined on the pew by a handsome dark-haired man whom she had never seen before. Her cheeks warm as she takes in the profile of his strong square jawline. She shifts in her seat and his gaze falls upon her. His full lips curl into an easy smile as he drinks her in.

She returns his smile and feels a familiar quiver dance through her. Her quim and mind are one, and a rush of heat pulses through her. She snakes her gaze along his body, taking in his broad shoulders and chest, until she reaches his waist. She watches in delight, and ponders the tactile effect of her stare, as he swells before her very eyes.

Upon instruction, they lower to the kneeler. Felicity, with eyes fixed forward, places her hand on his thigh. She can feel the heat of his skin felt through the soft gaberdine. Her hand traces along his leg, feeling the subtle flex and release of his muscle until she reaches the outline of his thickening member.

Felicity steals a quick glance from the corner of her eye as she passes her hand over the meat of him. His eyes flit to her direction then quickly refocuses ahead. Felicity closes her hand around him and grips him gently.

At first, she teases him with gentle pressure. Then, with determined rhythm, Felicity massages the lengthening bulge threatening to burst forth from his zipper.

Her unnamed paramour responds in kind. His large hand glides from Felicity's thigh to her hip. His fingers glide along her waist and he runs his flattened hand across the plain of her skirt to massage her sex in tempo with the ministrations of his cloaked cock.

His busy fingers gradually slip under her skirt and graze the damp gusset of her panties, eliciting a quiet sigh of contentment. Feeling the moist heat of her in his palm and observing the increasingly rapid rise and fall of her chest as she tried to contain her growing excitement, he continues to massage her through the thin satin and lace.

Inspired by her reaction, he slides a fingertip along the smooth material and applies direct pressure to her swollen nub.

Felicity draws her lower lip between her teeth and when she ventures to look at him, she is met with his passionate gaze. In his eyes she sees the intensity of her own hunger reflected.

She squeezes him and, with eyes locked, lowers his zipper.

She grazes her thumb across his swollen glans, and he responds with a ragged intake of breath. Felicity encircles him in her warm embrace and lowers his waistband as she slides her hand slowly up and down his thick, silky shaft.

With a quiet moan, he slips past her panties and dips a finger into her dripping heat.

She licks her lips. Under his intense gaze she feels desired and exposed. Her eyes mist as he slips another finger into her depths.

Pearls of excitement bead at his crown and she slips her thumb along his swollen head to gather his natural lubricant. Felicity's hand strokes and twists as she slides along his velvet shaft with increasing tempo. His breath, to her licentious, irreligious delight, was coming in quick, ragged gasps, and his glistening pearls now flowed freely.

Feeling his orgasm quickly approaching, he seeks to bring her to the brink with him. His thumb joins his teasing fingers. His thumb slips through her honey and circles her button. Slowly at first, then looping the bud with increasing speed and pressure.

His fingers piston in and out with increasing rhythm as her quim pulses around them, pressing his fingers, seeking to draw them deeper within her sodden treasure.

Her open mouth forms an "O", and her tongue runs along her lower lip, desperate to taste him.

His lust-hooded eyes stare into hers as his hips rock forward, pumping his velvety-steel rod through her slick, tight grip. He bares his clenched teeth and stifles a cry as his essence springs from his pulsing tip.

She watches him cum with hedonistic awe. Arch after arch surges forth from his fount to the glistening hardwood below, covering her hand and bubbling along her knuckles as she continues to pump her fist along his rock-hard prick.

His thumb strums her pearl faster and his fingers drive in and out of her pulsing quim as they search for the fulcrum of her desire.

Her raspy breath and muted mewls of need join the chorus of psalms as her pussy wrings her devotee's fingers. Felicity's orgasm crests and she feels her body begin to soar to the heavens.

Felicity keeps one hand on her lover's shaft as her other hand grips the top of the pew before her. Her vision momentarily blurs and her body freezes in an erotic tableau as his fingers unleash her passion. With a swipe of his thumb, a second seismic wave quakes through her and Felicity's body trembles with libidinous abandon as her fingers dig into the empty pew.

His digits slowly dip in and out until they skate along her parted, sopping lips. They then slip delicately passed her tingling, exposed nub and down her thighs, wet with her excitement. His hand is soaked with her spending, and he brushes his fingers over the light strip of hair atop her sex.

Felicity's thighs quiver with the aftershocks racing through her body and she releases her grip on the pew.

She continues to softly stroke the semi-erect cock in her hand and smiles, still caught in the blissful wash of orgasm. She raises the waistband of her mystery man's briefs and holds him in her embrace until he is snugly secure in his cotton enclosure, the sticky remains of his excitement surrounding him.

A voice breaks through their carnal reprieve, and they rise from their kneeler.

"Everyone, let us meet our neighbour. Please shake the hand of someone new," came the instruction of the Pastor.

They turn, each with their hand drenched in the nectar of the other.

"Peace be with you," Felicity says to her wanton consort. She feels a pulse ripple through her clit as a rivulet of syrup steals down her inner thigh.

"And also, with you." The heat in his eyes echoes the expanding need in his trousers.

The meeting of their honeyed hands sparks lust anew, and the two strangers, now closer than friends, slip away to the rectory for a proper introduction.

New Leaf

I had my earbuds in as I walked down the street. My hair was tied into a ponytail high on the top of my head and my long black curly hair hung in loose ringlets passed my shoulders to the center of my back. The music was so engrossing that I didn't notice at first, but my hips were swaying in time with the tunes as I walked unhurried down the street to nowhere in particular.

I had just moved back to my hometown and was reacquainting myself with the sights and sounds of the neighbourhood. Not much had changed in the ten years since I was away at school. The one thing that had changed was the people I had gone to high school with and the folks that I knew. We all got a little bit older, a little bit wiser in our own way. It was refreshing.

I popped into the local corner store and ran into my neighbour when I was growing up. We exchanged delighted hellos and made promises to catch up soon. I wonder how much sincerity was in that brief conversation. Not much on my part, if I'm being honest. I had become somewhat aloof when I was away and that didn't seem to get me very far outside the city. I would have to work on that.

Turn over a new leaf and all that.

I was heading in the general direction of my old high school. It was at the bottom of a hill and a dead-end street. It was almost poetic how much people wanted to get out of there and move on with their lives. And here I was, back in town, and heading directly down that hill. I smiled to myself and gave my head a subtle shake. My hair danced around my bare shoulders. My red halter tank displayed my sun-kissed, toned arms and formed delicately along my sides, flat stomach and high, pert breasts. My indigo denim skirt hugged my hips and gently flared just below the swell of my plump ass. The rhythmic sway of my hips gave any onlookers quick tiny peeks at my smooth mocha globes as I bopped down the street.

I reached the school and took a quick tour around the grounds and remembered what it was like to be a big fish in this little pond.

It was intoxicating to recall what it felt like to be young and excited about everything. I began to feel flushed as I recalled certain naughty memories of my wild youth; the corners where I hid away to suck a dick, or fuck.

My panties began to dampen as I thought about the times when I was tangled in desire and would cry out in ecstasy, hoping no one would walk by and catch us. I may have been a little naughty back in high school. Maybe.

I walked past the tennis courts and watched a lesson in progress. I stood at the high chain link that fenced in the six courts, to observe more closely.

The instructor looked vaguely familiar to me, but it was hardly his face that I was interested in. His legs were beautiful. Well muscled and tanned. His collared polo shirt clung to his pecs and what appeared to be a washboard stomach as his body was drenched with sweat.

My breath became shallow as I watched his body move. I thought of those hot trysts I had all around the school grounds and listened to the punctuated pop of the green tennis ball against the racket and the players grunting their effort upon connection, and my mind swirled with desire.

I must have been staring, for when I refocused my gaze on the instructor, I could see a slight smirk across his face as he approached.

Stepping back from the fence, I locked eyes with him and licked my lips.

Sweat had begun to bead on my chest, and it slowly dripped down to the recess of my cleavage. The sensation caused my nipples to harden and strain against the thin material of my shirt. I watched his hungry gaze take in the knots that formed on the tips my swollen breasts and responded with a libidinous smile.

I heard the smart pock of the racket connecting to the ball and the echo of the ball and the squeak of shoes as his students raced to claim it. It bounced to a stop on the court, and I heard him call to them.

Their lesson was over, but another, all together different one, was about to begin.

I shivered under the hot August sun and walked away from the court. I turned back toward the building, and I leaned against the rusty coloured brick, awaiting his arrival.

His students slowed as they walked past me, taking a look at the woman who had so abruptly halted their lesson. I had never seen them before, but I was sure, given the depth of their study as they passed, they would never forget me.

I smiled at them. It was a quick pressing of my lips and a brief lifting of my eyebrows in amused acknowledgment. They tried to be subtle about it as they looked me the up and down. The one thing teenaged boys lacked was subtly. They both drank in my shapely legs and almost too short skirt. I felt their eyes survey the rest of my body as I turned my head away from them in general disinterest. I had other thoughts on my mind that had nothing to do with the lust-filled, open-mouthed stares of adolescents.

I turned up the volume on my music and closed my eyes. He would be along shortly, and I was getting impatient. Being back in that space reminded me of how wild I had been. It awakened a familiar uncontrollable hunger that I had long since put away. Being here again unhinged the place deep inside me that held my desire. I was very much looking forward to reliving those not so innocent days of my youth.

I felt more than saw him approach. I could smell his masculine dampness as his body come closer to mine. I tilted my face upward toward his and smiled. It was a devious smile. I did recognize him. He was one of those guys I saw in high school who would peer through the windows of the library, fascinated at the brazen activity that took place in the courtyard right outside the window. Front and centre of the show was yours truly. I recognized the almond shape of his eyes that grew large between a slit in the curtains as I wrapped my lips around a plump nipple or purple knob.

He had certainly filled out since those days. He stood nearly a head taller than my delicate 5 feet 4 inches. His almond shaped eyes were a translucent hazel colour, and they were lit with determination and wanting. He looked at me like a man starved and I the waiting banquet.

I licked my lips in response to his molten gaze. I felt my pussy dampen and pulse with anticipation.

His pink lips were parted slightly, and his breath was coming in a shallow rhythm as I pulled seductively at the frayed hem of my denim skirt.

His white polo still clung to his body, and closer, I could now see the faint tangle of dark hair that graced his lower abdominals that led their way to delights below the waistband of his matching white tennis shorts.

I watched as his mouth moved. He was saying something, but I didn't want to hear anything from him. We both knew why we were there. Why delay it with mindless chit chat?

"Shhh," I said and pointed to my ears. "I have my earbuds in. I can't hear you." I gave a coy flip of my hair and batted my eyelashes at him innocently.

He gave me a strange look and for a moment didn't seem to know what to do. He stepped back hesitantly, as though he had read the signs incorrectly. He had not. His body knew why he was there. Of that there was no doubt.

I smiled and lowered my eyes to the expanse etched in the front of his shorts. His thick and growing erection pressed against the zipper aching for release. My mouth watered in anticipation of feeling his heavy tool against my lips.

I looked down at my ripe breasts and encircled them with my hands, watching the pupils in his hazel eyes widen. I slipped the red material over my heaving chest and lowered my lips to my upturned nipple. He watched me, transfixed as my tongue swirled around my delicate nubs and I cooed softly as I took them in my mouth in turn, leaving them slick with my saliva.

I tossed the garment on the ground and brought my hands to the waistband of his shorts, and I pulled him closer. My thumbs did a quick pass over his hardness, and I sighed in delight.

This was going to be fun.

I put my palms flat on his chest and traced along his fine muscular body. I tilted my head to the side and invited his lips to my neck. He kissed me there, gently at first, then his kisses grew hungrier, more desperate.

I let my hands roam his body; his chest, down to his defined abdomen, where I counted the ridges of his washboard stomach. His teeth nipped at my throat as he lavished me with kisses. My breath was coming in increased sighs. I wanted to shift this passion play into high gear.

My hands slipped under his shirt and ran along his kinetic skin. I could feel every muscle alive with sexual energy. Frantically, I removed his shirt and tossed it beside my crumpled tank on the ground.

He took my face in his hands and brought my lips to meet his. The connection was electric; his tongue immediately dueled with mine.

I sucked on his thrashing tongue and felt his tickle the underside of my own. Our kiss was deep and audacious. Our hands roamed freely along each other's naked torso.

His fingers danced up and down my spine and slid playfully along my ribs until they came to rest on my bountiful C cups. He gently squeezed and fondled them, grazing his thumbs over their peaks. The sensation of him thumbing my nubs brought fuel anew to my internal fire.

The track on the song changed and a pulsing beat claimed my pussy. I wanted to taste him.

I sunk to my knees before him and brought down his rasping zipper with care. His hot meat lay tense beneath the thin cotton layer of his underwear. Without ceremony, I drew them down, my mouth open and waiting for his cock to spring, loaded and ready for action, onto my waiting tongue.

His veiny, silky prick was as thick as his tight clothing implied. I reached out for his shaft and began a slow process of sliding my hands up and down his shaft. The bulbous tip lay on my tongue while I worked my hands along his rigid shaft.

I closed my lips around the head of his meaty schlong. I ran my tongue around the glans, where shaft met head and along the large head to where he was leaking the most delicious pre-cum I had tasted in quite some time.

I listened to the tunes playing in my ears, and I felt the excitement building in his ever-expanding prick.

His cock was dribbling steadily onto my tongue, and I swallowed the nectar down as I pumped my hands up and down his shaft. One hand reached lower and felt the weight of his neatly manscaped sac. I rolled his balls around my hand, feeling him shift and move as I increased the pressure of my suckling mouth.

His fingers were in my hair in a vain attempt to control my pace and manipulations of his organ. He tried to hold me still while he fucked my mouth, but I wouldn't let him. I was in control. I would set the pace.

I held my hand firmly against his hip and slowly began to move forward, allowing his thick cock to travel the length of my tongue. I wrapped my tongue around him and sucked while I bobbed my head at a deliciously slow pace up and down his meat. His prick touched the back of my throat, and I slowed even further. I relaxed and opened my throat to accommodate his size. His long, thick cock nestled in my throat, and my nose buried against his sculpted pelvis.

I took my time with him, easing him down my throat and out again, flicking the tip of my tongue along his sensitive head and slurping him down whole again.

I felt his hips arching forward as he tried to increase the pace. His ball sack became heavier, and I could feel him pulsating in my mouth. His lips were curled into a snarl and his chest rose and fell in rapid succession. He was on the brink, and I wanted all of it.

Looking into his eyes, I swallowed him whole once more and gave his balls a gentle squeeze. His face filled with wonder as his cock rocketed out its first long rope of jizz, directly into my belly.

He pulsed and continued to spurt more of his manly essence down my willing throat. On the third spasm, I had brought the tip into my mouth. I wanted to taste his cream, to feel its silkiness in my mouth before I swallowed. He was delicious, rich, and creamy.

Breathless, he watched as I reached under my skirt and pulled off my lacy G-string. Sexy and red, it matched my tank, and like my tank, it would grace the concrete steps behind us.

It was my turn to be breathless.

I stood up and leaned back against the brick. The tender skin of my back felt every notch and crevice of the 40-year-old building.

Licking the errant drips of cum from the corners of my lips, I watched as he took up my former position. I relished in how he looked, on his knees, before me, prepared to worship at the shrine of Venus.

His hands smoothed over the naked globes of my tight ass. He held them, squeezed, and fondled them. He drew his fingers along the underside, where cheek met leg and followed along to my hips. He traced this circuit a number of times, all the while not breaking eye contact with me, dipping his fingers ever closer on each pass, to the treasures waiting just further still.

His fingertips dipped between my thighs, coming away damp and sticky with my excitement.

Dipping his fingers back again, he touched the fluttering opening to my wetness. He brought his fingers to his lips and held my gaze as he painted his tongue with my juice.

Pulling my legs wider apart, his head disappeared beneath the short denim of my skirt. I smiled to myself, amused, as I peered down to look like what might as well have been a small jean hat atop his head. My smile was replaced by a groan as I felt his tongue slide along my labia, sending electric charges through my body.

My stomach fluttered as I felt his lips take each of my pussy lips between them and suckle upon them gently.

I rolled up the miniature amount of material to what could be fashioned a belt and watched as his mouth slipped all around my delightfully wet pussy.

His tongue reached out and slid along my dripping gash. He curled his tongue to receive every ounce of offering from my dripping quim. I could feel him hum in delight as his tongue slipped passed my gates and scooped a mouthful of my ecstasy.

Sensations washed through my body as his tongue languidly feasted on my pussy. My eyes closed tight, and my back arched off the wall when I felt his fingers join his delicious mouth as they pried apart my swollen lips and he drove his tongue deep into the recesses of my treasure.

Lapping with increased vigor I panted against his ministrations. His tongue lashed out and struck my sensitive bud. I howled at the sensation. "More!" I cried. "Yes, yes, yes," I chorused as my hips did a tight loop, ensuring his tongue did not lose contact with my clitty. The complex tangle of nerves sparked and quaked as he pointed his tongue and flicked against my button again and again.

I couldn't know how loud I was; my music was blasting in my ears. It was as though my playlist knew the activities I was engaged in and ensured I had a soundtrack to get off to.

My eyes flew open as I felt my orgasm rapidly approach. He was doing everything right. My knees began to shake, and I pressed my mons on his slick face.

His lips closed over my throbbing clit, and he began to suck.

I screamed wordlessly as he alternated between sucking and flicking my nub with his tongue. My juices drenched his face and spilled down his neck.

I was still reeling from my incredible spend and I watched his fabulously talented tongue gather my excitement from my thighs and above and below his full lips.

We locked eyes as he smiled up at me, his throat bobbing as he swallowed my nectar.

He rose before me and planted a hot passionate kiss on my lips. My tongue immediately searching his mouth, tasting myself on his lips and purring in delight at the sweetness of my honey pot.

His hands were tight on my hips and in one motion, almost as though we were dancing, he spun me around to face the wall.

I looked back over my shoulder and bit my lip as I took in his eyes, hooded with desire, staring at my quaking buttocks. He tilted my hips and my ass arched higher in the air. I could feel the delicate breeze tickling the spare hair covering my yoni. I could feel my quim puckering, hungry lips awaiting his steely manhood.

Rock music began to play. It was high energy and up tempo, yet there was something wholly animalistic about it. It was full of yearning and desire. I don't know if that was the intention, but the rifts and chords that echoed in my ears did nothing but ratchet up my lust and make me hunger for more.

His cock, hard and long, lay like a spear between us. The hot tip of his shaft slid through the puddle of my wetness again and again as he prepared himself to take me.

I wiggled my ass back at him, no longer willing to wait for him to pierce my honied gates and fill me; and yet, he made me wait.

He lubed himself up in my juice and ran his steel shaft along my oversexed clitty. I chewed my lower lip and dropped my head forward, gurgling in excitement.

I felt him draw his long cock back against my nub and position the bulbous head of his prick at my drooling slit. I braced my hands against the wall and felt his hands grip my hips.

"Ahhhh!" I called out to the heavens as I felt his massive cock plunge through my gates and fill me to the brim. He held there for a moment and my cunney squeezed around him like a hand milking him. It sucked his thick cock in its tight sheath, and he pulled out slowly. I felt my soft lips suck on its delicious lollipop and release as he pulled completely out.

Momentarily at a loss, my hands caressed my breasts. I brought my nipples to my mouth and licked them in turn. My mouth sucking on my sensitive knot when he crashed through my cunney lips.

My pussy spurt hot nectar and lathered our joint sex as he thrust forward again, this time angling his rod along the elusive tangle of nerves inside.

The explosion of colour and sound that emitted surprised us both and he wavered in his stroke, riding deeper inside and sawing deliciously on my G-Spot.

"Oh God! Right there!"

My call was heard directly in my pussy. My walls quivered and wrung his rod as he pistoned his hips, drawing back so that only his swollen helmet remained, then riding forward again.

His pace quickened. We would not be able to maintain this cresting pleasure for long.

"Welcome to my world, she said." The heavy strum of the guitar stings reverberated as the molasses voiced singer dripped hungrily in my ears.

I gasped as he thrust his hips forward, the tip of his hot cock striking the opening of my womb and his heavy balls slapped against my soaking hot sex.

I could feel his sweat dripping down onto my arched back and I looked back to see the fury with which he hammered his thick cock into my juicy nook.

"Uhhh. Yes!" I cried, feeling his thick tool drag through my sucking lips. I threw my head back, dislodging one of my earbuds and exposing me to the incredible sounds he was making while he pounded my sopping pussy.

My cunney clenched on his thick prick as I heard him panting. The pock sound from the tennis court was now replaced by the sound of his flesh slapping hard against my own.

"Fuck," he grunted as he reared above me once more and slammed into my quim.

A warbling sound emitted from my throat as I responded with passion. My hips raced back to meet his next thrust, and his fingers dug into my tender flesh.

"Uummm! Ghhhh!" he grunted, and his hips moved ever faster. Hearing him on the verge of flooding me was too much for my blazon quim.

"Fuuuuuuck!" I screamed. "Yes! Flood me! Yes!" My honey pot held his veiny member. I could feel him swelling inside me as my command rang out.

"Uuuuuuuggh!" His hips crashed to mine, and he held me tight.

My thighs flattened against his, and his cock, buried in the deepest recesses of my cunney, exploded.

My own orgasm burst forth. Stars sparked across my vision, and I screamed nonsense words to the open field of the collegiate institute.

My excitement sprayed forth, soaking his hips, and dousing his light sprinkle of hair.

He brought his hands forward to capture my breasts and I leaned back against his sweat-slicked body. Our sex joint and trembling as he shot blast after blast of hot cum into my quaking pussy.

Breathing deeply and still pressed together in the dampness of our libidinous act, he pulled me down to the ground. His cock had only begun to soften slightly, and our bodies were still coupled. He caressed my tits and traced a rivulet of sweat between my heaving chest down my belly to my sticky sex.

Moving onto my knees, I held him tight within me as he drew slick circles around my extended bud.

I felt him stir within me as his lightening rod began to swell to its previous glory. My pussy responded with a squeeze and delightfully wet squelch.

I looked over at my earbuds, discarded on the concrete, and thought, the sound of his ramrod pace and the echo of his tenor as he came, was the only music I needed.

I closed my eyes as I rocked my hips back and forth seductively, feeling him stir our mutual essence inside me.

"Mmmm, yeah," he sighed and drew in a deep breath.

The tips of his fingers alternated between stiff and fluttering against my clitty. My chest rose and fell in pace with his torturous play.

Yeah, this was going to be a good day.

I may have moved back to turn over a new leaf, but sometimes, it's just the other side of the old one.

Primal Beat

Sound reverberated off slick cavern walls. The party was in full swing. Bodies writhed to the rhythm and bare feet slapped the puddles of water pooled indiscriminately around them.

I looked at the invitation and smiled. Who sends actual invitations anymore? It was a novelty and an homage to a time long passed. It added to the intrigue, and I very much looked forward to the evening.

My Uber driver pulled into the near deserted parking lot and caught my eyes in the rear-view mirror as though to say, 'Are you sure?'

I responded with a wink and left the car.

I walked down the boardwalk to where the park met wilderness and continued to a staircase hidden in the dunes.

The staircase led down to the bottom of the cliff face and nestled in the rock there was a large door. Affixed to the door was a heavy iron knocker in the shape of a lion's face. A large metal ring pierced through the nostrils of the feline and a square sat at the bottom. I raised the heavy iron knocker and rapped twice on the door, as instructed by the invitation.

The heavy wooden door opened, and I stepped inside the threshold. The light was dim and there was a slight humidity in the air. It was a stark change from the crisp and cool autumn night. Music was playing. It was soft and inviting and seemed to come from nowhere in particular and yet permeated everywhere.

The walls were adorned with heavy tapestries and where one did not hang, the walls had been painted a luxurious red colour with golden flecks scattered throughout.

The man who opened the door, now stood aside and watched as I settled in the new environment. I watched him as he watched me. He was tall, perhaps six foot three, and well built. He had a frame that was finely dressed in a butler outfit that must have been tailor made. There wasn't a stich out of place, not a piece of cloth that did not accentuate the breadth of his chest or leave much to the imagination as to his masculine prowess.

Silently, the butler led me down the hall. The only sound was that of my heels clacking against the textured grey slate floor. He pointed me to a cloak room and upon review of my invitation, told me that once inside I was to look for the number that appeared at the bottom right of the card.

Once inside, I noticed that there were more than coats on hangers. Entire outfits hung neatly in small open cupboards, like the ones from grade school. And just like grade school, at the bottom of the cubby were pairs of "outside shoes". At the bottom of mine were a pair of slippers.

I stepped out of my shoes and shrugged my jacket off my shoulders. I placed my jacket on a hanger and looked over my shoulder, suddenly shy.

I unbuttoned my burgundy satin sleeveless blouse and pulled it off. I caught a glimpse of myself in the mirror and drew my hands along my curves. My breasts were nestled high in a black satin demi bra. My fingertips glided over the slippery material. It was a subtle contrast to the silkiness of the swell of my breasts. Content, I smiled and removed my bra and hung it alongside my blouse.

My fingers traced my curves as I became more aware of the music that dripped from speakers hidden in the walls and ceiling. It seemed to be coming from everywhere and nowhere at the same time. The sensual draw of bow on strings wrapped luxuriously around me and drew erotic imaginings in my mind. My fingers danced along my skin, leaving a trail of raised flesh in its wake.

The tingling trail led to my hip and the zipper of my skirt. I drew tiny circles along my waist, teasing and exciting my senses. I pulled the zipper downwards and the structured denim fell to my feet.

I stepped out of the skirt and smoothed my hands over my bare legs. Bent at the waist I undid the buckles nestled against my ankles and stepped out of my wedge heels.

Turning back to the mirror, I smiled. There was no reason for me to feel embarrassed. My eyes lingered on my frame for a moment longer and with a quiet sigh, I pulled the robe from the hanger and slipped my feet into the slippers and opened the door to the cloakroom to step back into the hall.

The butler stood a few feet away and gave me a welcome smile, noting that I was a few inches shorter than when I came into the large tucked away mansion.

He walked two strides ahead of me and led me down a narrow corridor and a short flight of stairs. The air in the hall had changed. It was different in this new area of the house. It was humid and there was a touch of saltiness to it. And the music had changed. No longer were there soft, delicate strings. A subtle and persistent drumbeat had taken its place. The combination was almost primal, and I began to feel carried away.

He gestured to a small room off the hallway. "Take off your robe and slippers in there, then go through the door on the opposite side of the room. Follow the music and have a great time."

"Thanks," I replied. I felt tiny butterflies flitting around in my stomach as the door closed behind me.

I accepted an invitation to an exclusive party and have spent most of the time since I arrived, alone, and prepping for the event. It was almost showtime and I was beginning to get nervous. What was behind that door?

I peeled the robe from my shoulders and placed it on a hook and put the slippers directly underneath them. I strode to the door, my nude body tingling with anticipation. I opened the door.

When I stepped through that door, any semblance of the house I had walked through fell away. I was surrounded by stone. The tapestries that hung in the halls of the elaborate and luxurious mansion were replaced by the chaos and beauty of chiseled rock. The floor that once was slate was now the same stone as the wall. Its tone the shade of an auburn sunset interspersed with pinks and onyx, and random sparkles of amethyst. As I walked through the wide tunnel I felt pulled forward as though some invisible force called to me – a force which would not be ignored.

The muted thump of the primal drums increased in volume and became a rhythm that pulsed through the soles of my feet to the core of my body. I felt transported and followed the sound down a set of stone steps that rounded downward. The further I followed the stairs, the warmer and saltier the air became.

I began to hear the low murmur of voices and muted laughter.

Any coolness left in the air around me was now gone, replaced, as it was, by heat and moisture, almost as though I was entering a sauna. Beads of dew began to cling to my skin.

I could see light coming from the end of the hall and when I approached it a swell of excitement flooded through my body.

I stepped up to the wrought iron Juliette balcony embedded in the rock face and looked out at the unbelievable scene before me.

Anchored high in the ceiling were hundreds of candles placed in ornate iron candelabras. In the far corner was an iron cauldron sitting atop a perch. The cauldron had exquisite designs carved along its large bowl. Light flickered and flared, throwing strange shadows across the floor and walls from the fire that burned in its belly. The flecks of light seemed to be in tempo with the music that I could see now was being played by live musicians situated on a terrace similar to the one upon which I stood.

The shirtless muscular drummers banged their oversized percussive instruments and lithe bodies of dancers on the makeshift stage responded in turn.

I marvelled at the scene that stretched out impossibly before me. A sea of people rocked and churned en masse. Their bodies glistening and athletic, moved to and fro as they danced. Each person, naked and uninhibited.

I yearned to be part of their dance. Their freedom.

I turned away from the scene and continued down the tunnel, toward the music and the dancers.

Toward the fire.

The staircase I descended was carved in stone and the closer I got to the bottom, the cooler the steps became under my feet and the louder the music became. I stood at the threshold, naked and shivering with anticipation. I knew that this event would be the beginning of a new chapter for me. I knew I could never go back to the life I had led before.

I crossed the threshold and entered the arena. I was welcomed by eyes that caressed my body and smiles that caressed my soul. I smiled back at those who caught my eye and my hand was taken hold of by a woman with red hair that fell down her back in thick luxurious waves and rested on the firm rise of her buttocks.

The ivory of her skin was sprinkled with freckles and when she turned back to face me, her eyes were a brilliant emerald that sparkled with mischief and excitement.

She had chosen me out of the crowd, and we were carried forward on a wave and I found myself surrounded by the sweat dampened bodies of revellers.

Breasts and buttocks shook and swayed before me in a dizzying dance. My own body responded to the incessant percussion. My hips twisted to and fro and my arms were raised above my head while my hands swayed. I could feel the ground beneath my bare feet, and I felt centered and connected, a feeling I had not experienced in a very long time. I closed my eyes and let myself surrender to the true primal nature of the atmosphere.

My senses were heightened, and my skin bloomed with goose bumps when I felt my red-haired companion draw her hand along my raised arm, down my armpit and along my ribs. Her fingers tickled along my hip and she wrapped her arm around my waist and brought me closer.

The plain of our bellies kissed as she lined her hips up to mine. I looked down at our connected bodies and watched a trail of sweat drip from my breast and join the glistening wetness of our skin where it pressed together. I placed my hand on the flat of the small of her back and ground my hips onto hers as the sensation to possess her in the dance took me over.

My skin was alive with sensation. My adrenaline was pumping, and my excitement had begun to spark desire. My mind was flooded with elicit cravings with every motion of our bodies. Every time our skin grazed against one another desire surged forward. Goosebumps covered my exquisite nudity.

She pressed her chest to mine with a wet smack and slithered across my chest. Her left hand grasped onto my hip and her left hand traveled across my hip to my pert derriere, where she glided her hand along the curve of my ass to my thigh. She grasped my thigh and slid her hand sensuously to my knee and with a fluid motion, she brought my knee up to her hip, exposing my excited quim to the heat and electricity of the room.

I leaned back into her arms and settled my wetness on her hip. She pulled me tighter to her and I ground my sopping pudenda against her overheated skin.

I drew in a sharp breath as I felt her fingers graze my sensitive pouting lips. I pulled my lower lip between my teeth and shifted my hips forward, encouraging her long, delicate fingers to slip inside.

Her right hand lay flat against my back and pressed me ever closer to her. I watched her with a freedom and a fascination I had never known. I had never been with a woman before and to surrender myself this way to one so skillful with just her touch, I knew my lack of experience would be no hinderance. This night was about giving myself over, mind and body to the pure joy of our baser instincts and desires and I would experience everything the night had to offer.

She leaned forward, gazing into my eyes. Her eyes reflected humorous fascination. I watched her lips as she leaned down and closed my eyes when her lips planted a kiss on my neck. I was breathless and paralyzed. Her tongue traced the line from my earlobe to my collarbone and back again. She closed her lips over my earlobe and sucked it for a moment, then nipped it gently with her teeth.

The sensation sent a pulse through my core and settled deliciously in my pussy. I needed more.

The world fell away in that moment and there was just her and the delightful control she had over me.

I felt the tip of her fingers slip along my juicy snatch and strum lightly over my clit.

She flicked her finger over my button until I was weak and mewling with desire.

She released my leg and brought her fingers to my lips. I tasted the tart juices of my cunney on her slim digits and I licked them with vigor.

Around us, I could hear the sighs and groans of others entangled in their own amorous exercise. The sound of bodies slapping together added a libidinous undercurrent to the thumping of the primal drums.

I took the lead and explored her nimble body with my hands. I tickled them down her sides and came to rest on the fair, freckled swell of her breasts. My thumbs flicked lightly across the stiff knots of her nipples, and she threw her head back as I kissed my way down her chest to her upturned titties.

I took each nub between my lips and suckled and nipped them as she had done my earlobe. Her fingers danced around my shoulders and a series of deep melodic coos emerged from her throat in response.

She brought my face to her own and kissed me with a fiery passion. Our bodies, constantly in motion, flowed together to the rhythm of the drum, heightening our eager appetites. Yearning to touch and taste, we moved through the crowd of slick, nude bodies, until we came upon the stone-hewn stage upon which dancers strut and swayed.

With my mouth glued to hers, my red-haired maven positioned me against the raised rock face and toyed her fingers through the sparse thicket of hair covering my mons, finding my clitty and with delightful pressure, frigged my delicious button until I could no longer contain the spark and flood of my fast-building orgasm.

My eyes closed against the fireworks that burst forth in my mind; my tongue licked my salty lips. I was gasping for breath when the stiff pressure of her digits was replaced by the soft heat of her lips.

I opened my eyes to the new and tantalizing sensation and saw that she was on her knees before me. My fingers combed through her hair as her tongue slid deftly through my folds and collected the nectar deposited by the first of many exquisite climaxes that evening.

I felt myself racing toward another delightful orgasm. I kneaded my breasts and rolled my hard nipples between my thumbs and forefingers as her tongue fucked my heated pussy.

She held my lips open with the fingers of her one hand and exposed my engorged, sensitive clit to her lingual assault. I fought to close my thighs around her head as I gasped and moaned in pleasure, but she kept me open to her hungry mouth and I could do nothing but submit.

My mouth was slack as I panted and called out my passion. I squeezed my titties and brought my tongue to my elongated nipples and licked them fervently.

Resigned to her skill, I gave myself over and my orgasm flooded her mouth. Her tongue lashed and flared through my climaxing cunney, and my mouth was opened in a silent scream that shook me to the core.

Panting and vulnerable, I felt her take another long sweep from my ass to clit, and settling there, she patiently drew out my quivering bud, extending an already knee-buckling orgasm. Delirious with passion, I watched as she, on her knees before me, suckled my delicate clit between soft and persistent lips.

My cunney erupted with a fresh spurt of honey and my eyelids squeezed tight as the incredible waves of my spending echoed throughout my body. I was cast adrift on ecstasy.

My breath came in short gasps and my body tingled from the tips of my fingers to my toes. When I opened my eyes, the world was a blur. The first to find me, the pulsing beat of drums thrumming my core, centering me, guiding me back to the moment.

Looking down, the sweat dripping down my chest and across the plain of my belly came into focus, the sounds of sex floated to my ears, the humid air heavy with the salt of exertion. Lovers in the near distance fucked and sucked with abandon.

My companion was gone. Alone in a sea of smut, I was left with a satisfied smile and a desire to return the favour.

I looked around and spotted a raven-haired goddess rising from the crowd, her small breasts heaving upon her chest as she cried out. I approached her and slipped a finger into her naked treasure.

She ground her juicy vulva against my upturned palm as I wiggled my middle finger in her depths.

I dropped to my knees and laved my tongue through her wetness. Her taste a mix of sweet and savoury. The ambrosia of her desire mixed with the masculine essence of the lover who left her in the throes, ripe for my picking, played upon my tongue.

I held her wild gaze, wrapping my arms around her hips, pulling her tighter to me as I darted my tongue past her swollen petals into her heat.

She tangled her hands through my hair, her hips a blur as she ground her sopping pussy against my lips, seeking to ride my tongue as her screeching orgasm hit. Arching her hips toward the colossal chandeliers, she erupted on my chin and suckling mouth, bathing me in the force of her orgasm. Undeterred, I swallowed delicious mouthfuls of her delicacy and lay upon her quaking thigh, pausing a moment between errant licks of her silky lips to catch my breath.

The crowd stirred, pulling me away from my raven-haired temptress. Where my lips once graced was now a large cock. I watched in fascination as strong tawny hands lifted and lowered her upon his rigid tool.

I licked my lips and was surprised and delighted to meet a nipple, the colour of chestnut. I looked to my right to find a beautiful woman with springing black curls, lips spread to accommodate the mahogany member slipping down her willing throat.

The crowd shifted again. My melanin-kissed seductress found herself of her hands and knees, her lips and tongue working the veiny shaft gliding in and out of her full mouth. Straddling me, my lips never leaving her toasted rubies, she reaches down and gently pinches and taunts my excited clitty.

I twist beneath her and coax her molten treasure to my lips and tongue below. A gasp from her allows a droplet of precum to spill from her lips to my desperate sex below. Her sucking mouth, stretched wide, dribbles her saliva and his seed upon my wanton box.

Pulling her spicy cunney to my mouth, I thrust my tongue deep and was met with the electric sensation of another tongue skating along mine, lapping her sweetness.

Rocking back and forth, our curly-haired playmate ground her clit into my mouth, while my partner-in-cunnilingus probed her pussy's depths with his very skillful tongue. His long, swollen cock swayed like a pendulum beneath him as he revelled in her juicy snatch.

Drawing nearer, he brough his creamy cock into my waiting mouth. I wrapped my tongue around the tip and sucked him deeper into my mouth. I watched with building hunger as he dipped first one, then two fingers into her slattern honeypot, increasing his pace as he slowly fed his cock to me.

Arcing my neck, I allowed the tip of his velvety cock to touch the back of my throat, a slow pistoning of his hips, allowing me to bring him deeper and deeper into my willing throat. A chorused primal grunt from our gentlemen encouraged a joint celebratory suckle upon our respective clits before we returned to their meaty offerings.

I took turns flicking my tongue against her stiff bud and snaking my tongue around his hot shaft, her hips lolling in rhythm to our coordinated movements.

I lifted my hips to meet her dripping, moaning mouth. Large hands gripped my ass and raised me higher, supporting me as the heaviness of her playmate's cock lay slick against my pussy. Her lips and tongue joined his heat as they set about my clit, pleasing and teasing me. I could feel her simpering moans echo through me as she ran her tongue over my clit and his cock in unison.

Her mewling moans became more urgent as my lover, rushing to his peak pulled his long prick from my lips and slipped into her waiting pussy.

Not to be outdone, the fat, steely cock teasing my clitty pressed through my pouting lips, drawing from me an extended, wavering cry as I crested and delivered myself up to the goddess of desire once more.

My curly-haired concubine drowned me in her lust as our lovers came in succession, covering us with rope after rope of their animal vigor.

The crowd stirred once more, moving in time to the primal beat. Bodies in motion, shadows dancing in the chaotic light, echoing and feeding upon one another's most craven desires.

My lips, sullied with nectar, was eager to take a sip from more honeyed vessels and the evening did not disappoint, providing multiple opportunities taste and to be tasted.

I left there exhausted, on unsure legs, and with a satisfied pussy as the sun began to rise over the lake.

I smiled at my Uber driver as he took me away from that mysterious cavern of debauchery and a tingle passed through my body and settled in the knot of my clit as I thought about the next time I might receive the invitation to join them for a wild night of exploration and lechery.

About the Author

Caycie Thompson is the author of scorching erotic tales and steamy writing prompts for those who write or aspire to write sultry erotic fiction.

She is the author of *69 Prompts for Writers of Erotica*, *The Jurist* series and her work is featured in "Forbidden: A Temptation Press Anthology".

Check out her website, cayciethompson.com, for writing prompts for writers of erotica seeking a little inspiration for their next sexy short story.

She works in the bustling metropolitan city of Toronto, Ontario and loves to write and relax at her home in rural Ontario, where she lives with her husband.

Read Caycie After Dark

Books

The Jurist: Courtroom Drama

The Jurist: Security Issues

69 Prompts for Writers of Erotica

Web

www.cayciethompson.com

Social Media

Facebook, Instagram & X: @WrittenbyCaycie